THE GLASS HEART

A tale of three princesses

SALLY GARDNER

Orion
Children's Books

In all the hustle and bustle of getting ready for Nana's birthday party, Rosie had been forgotten. She had wandered off to her Nana's bedroom, where she loved to look at all Nana's little things. Her favourite was the glass heart that lay on a velvet cushion, so delicate that Rosie was sure it had been made by the fairies.

Then something awful happened. Rosie had been told not to touch the glass heart, and she didn't mean to, but now it lay in pieces on the floor. Rosie burst into tears. She knew Nana loved the glass heart, and she would be so cross.

But Nana wasn't cross. "It doesn't matter. These things happen,"
she said. "Broken things can be mended so they're as good as new,
if not better." And she picked up the pieces and put them in a box.
"Did you know, Rosie, that some people have glass hearts? If they're
touched gently they ring out like silver bells, but if they are given a jolt
they can break in two."

"Like your glass heart," said Rosie.

"Sort of," said Nana. "Now, would you like me to tell you a story?"

"Oh, yes!" said Rosie. She cuddled up with Nana and listened to
the distant sounds of people putting out glasses for the party.

"Shall I begin?" said Nana.

ONCE, LONG AGO, there was a king and queen who lived in a city built on water.

"Why was it built on water?" asked Rosie.

"Because it was a magical city," said Nana.

They had three beautiful daughters who all had glass hearts.

"Children," said the queen, "you must take great care of your hearts.
They are very *fragile* and you are very *precious*."
So the girls did their best to stay out of harm's way.

But one day the eldest of the three princesses was looking out of the window when a grand boat passed by, carrying a prince. The princess's heart gave a leap of joy. Surely this was the prince of her dreams!

But the prince did not even notice her smiling down at him: he was too busy staring at his own reflection in the water, and seeing how handsome he looked.

The princess's heart went *p i n g*! The glass had broken, and she fell down quite dead.

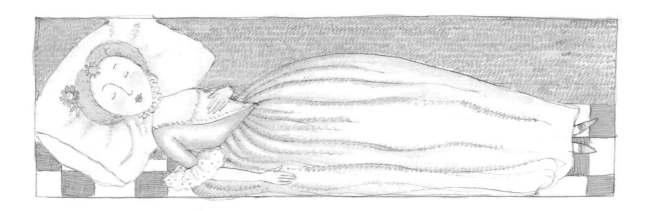

A little while later the second princess was walking in the garden and knelt down to smell a perfect pink rose. Its perfume was so gorgeous that her heart gave a *ting!* The glass had cracked, and she fell to the ground.

The king and queen ran to lift her up. They were overjoyed to see that she was all right. But a heart that is cracked has to be treated with care, or it will break in two. The princess, who was a very brave girl, told her parents not to fuss. She would lie by the window on a chaise longue and watch the world go by, with her little dog to keep her company.

"Sometimes hearts with cracks last even longer than hearts without," said the princess.

**A**LL THIS TIME the youngest princess was growing up. She was so beautiful, and so sweet and sensible, that everyone loved her. Many princes asked for her hand in marriage. But the king and queen were in no hurry to marry her off. A daughter with a glass heart should be careful who she falls in love with, in case her heart is broken.

"If she is to marry anyone," said the king, "he must not only be a prince, he must be good with glass as well."

But none of the princes knew anything about glass, so the king and queen had to turn them all away.

Now, the king had a handsome young page called Valentino, who was learning to be a courtier. One of his duties was to carry the princess's train, which he did very well. The princess liked the way he talked, and he was secretly in love with her.

One day the princess tripped. Valentino caught her effortlessly. Taking her hand,
he helped her to a chair. It was then that the princess noticed something about him.

"What?" asked Rosie.

"I'm not going to tell you now.
You'll have to wait and see," said Nana.

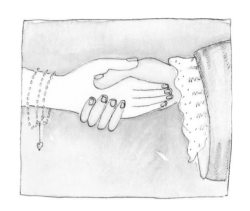

The king was so grateful that he gave Valentino a fine cloak as a reward.
"Now you are free to go out into the world and make your fortune," said the king,
"and I wish you all the best."

EVEN THOUGH Valentino's heart was not made of glass, he felt it would break if he had to leave the princess. She was sad too.

"If only you were a prince, and good with glass as well!" she sighed.

"There is nothing I can do to make myself a prince," said Valentino, "but I will learn all there is to know about glass, and then I will come back and try to win your hand."

Valentino took a gondola from the palace.

Then he sailed across the lagoon in a little boat

to an island not far away.

He went to see a glassblower he had heard of, who could make goblets and glasses and tiny glass animals so delicate that the slightest puff of wind would shatter them into a thousand pieces.

"Will you teach me all there is to know about glass?" asked Valentino.

"I will, but it will take three years," said the glassblower. "The first year you will have to get up early to fetch bread from the bakery, and look after the children. The second year you will learn how to make a fire hot enough to melt glass, and the third year I will teach you all there is to know."

Valentino was impatient. He wanted to get back quickly to his princess, so he asked if he could just do the last part. But the glassblower laughed and said, "Everything has to be done in the right order at the right time. Otherwise no good will come of it."

So the first year Valentino got up early to fetch the bread from the bakery and look after the glassblower's children.

The second year he learned how to make a fire hot enough to melt glass.

The third year he learned how to blow glass and model it,

and by the end of the year he had made three glasses, so delicate they looked as if they were made out of rainbows.

"They're fit for a king," said the glassblower.
"I have nothing more to teach you."

Valentino packed up the glasses
with great care, wrapped himself
in his fine cloak, and said
goodbye to the glassblower
and all his children.

Then he started on the long journey back to the city built on water, to see his princess.

BUT AS HE GOT CLOSER to the city, his courage failed him. Why would such a beautiful princess look twice at him? Surely by now she would have met and married a prince who was good with glass?

He was sitting by the roadside, his head in his hands, when a travelling circus passed by.

"Where are you going, and why so sad?" asked the clown.

Valentino told him about the princess with the glass heart.

"Well, you're in luck!" said the clown. "She hasn't found anyone to marry. Princes have come from far and wide but they knew nothing about glass and they were far too grand to be bothered to learn. So now the king is looking not for a prince, but for a man who is good with glass and two more things besides."

Valentino felt his heart would burst with joy.

"Do you know what these things are?" he asked.

"Yes," said the clown. "The princess must like
the young man, and he must have hands as soft
as velvet."

Valentino thanked the clown and
hurried on.

When he reached the city built on water, he found a long line of glaziers waiting outside the palace.

"What are glaziers?" asked Rosie.

"People who put the glass in windows," said Nana.

The princess had turned them all down, because although they knew a lot about glass their hands were rough from working with putty all day.

Valentino went up to the palace gates and asked to speak to the king. The guard knew him by his cloak and let him in.

Then Valentino presented the king with the three glasses. The king was most impressed, for it is difficult to carry anything so fragile without breaking it. He called for his daughter to come and look.

The princess was so happy to see Valentino again that a smile as bright as the sun spread over her face. She was delighted when he told her he had made the glasses himself.

"Oh papa, this is the man for me!" said the princess. "He is good with glass, and I know his hands are as soft as velvet." She had noticed that when she had tripped up.

The king and queen were happy that at last they had found the perfect young man for their daughter. There was a big wedding and a great masked ball, and the glassblower and all his children came, and so did the travelling circus.

V ALENTINO ALWAYS LOOKED AFTER his princess with great tenderness and care. They had many children and lived as happy as larks in the palace.

"What about the second princess, the one with the cracked heart?" asked Rosie.

"Well," said Nana...

The second princess still had to spend most of her time resting. She didn't mind because she had her little dog and her nephews and nieces, who thought she was the best auntie in the world. She told them stories, explained the stars to them, and wiped away their tears. Everyone loved her and she lived to a ripe old age in spite of the crack in her heart. She was fond of saying, "Well, my dears, that's the way it is: something that is broken and mended often lasts much longer than something that is new."

"Do you think she was right?" asked Rosie.

"Yes, I do. I remember when I was your age that
I dropped a pretty milk jug that my mother had, and it
cracked. My mother mended it very carefully, and it
has lasted ever since. Do you know, I still have it, and I
wouldn't exchange it for all the new milk jugs in the world.
Now," said Nana, "shall we go down and join the party?"